Toucan

Animals of the Amazon Rainforest

Katie Gillespie

EYEDISCOVER

EYEDISCOVER

Go to www.eyediscover.com and enter this book's unique code.

BOOK CODE

A 7 5 8 9 6 2

EYEDISCOVER brings you optic readalongs that support active learning.

Published by AV² by Weigl
350 5th Avenue, 59th Floor New York, NY 10118
Website: www.eyediscover.com

Library of Congress Control Number: 2016938328

ISBN 978-1-4896-4575-3 (hardcover)

Printed in the United States of America
in Brainerd, Minnesota
1 2 3 4 5 6 7 8 9 0 20 19 18 17 16

042016
041516

Editor: Katie Gillespie
Designer: Mandy Christiansen

Weigl acknowledges Getty Images, Corbis, and Shutterstock as the primary image suppliers for this title.

EYEDISCOVER provides enriched content, optimized for tablet use, that supplements and complements this book. EYEDISCOVER books strive to create inspired learning and engage young minds in a total learning experience.

I am a lion.

Watch
Video content brings each page to life.

Browse
Thumbnails make navigation simple.

Read
Follow along with text on the screen.

Listen
Hear each page read aloud.

Your EYEDISCOVER Optic Readalongs come alive with...

Audio
Listen to the entire book read aloud.

Video
High resolution videos turn each spread into an optic readalong.

OPTIMIZED FOR

☑ **TABLETS**

☑ **WHITEBOARDS**

☑ **COMPUTERS**

☑ **AND MUCH MORE!**

Toucan

In this book, you will learn about

- how I look

- where I live

- what I eat

and much more!

I am a tropical bird.
I am known for my large
bill and bright colors.

7

My bill can be red, yellow, orange, white, or green. Its colors help to keep me safe.

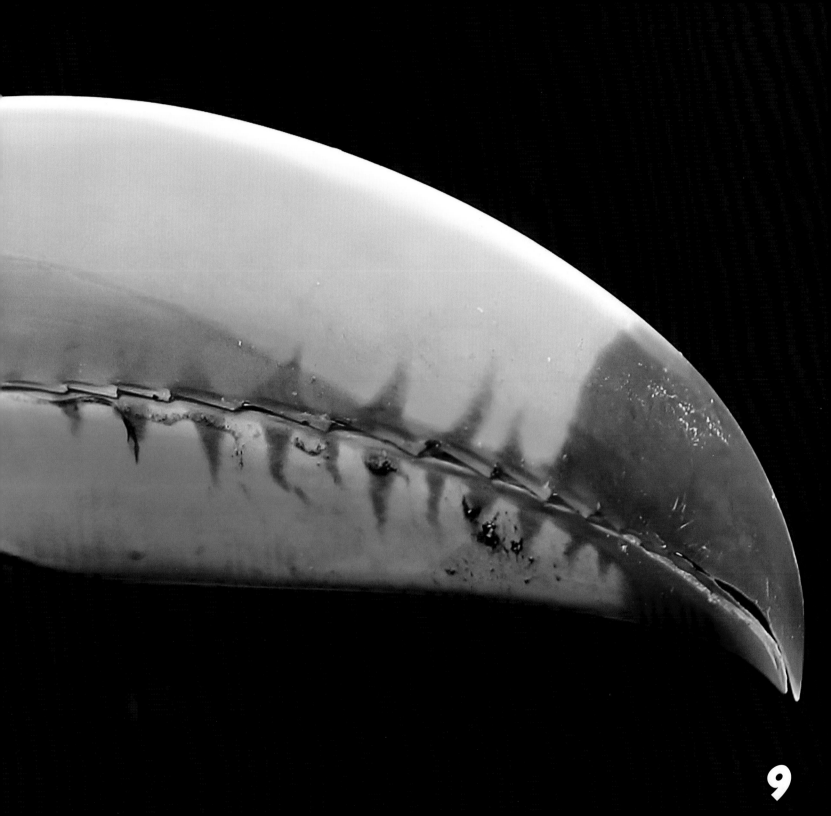

9

My bill has sharp edges just like teeth. I use them to catch and peel my food.

I eat mostly fruit. Sometimes I also eat bird eggs, lizards, nuts, or seeds.

13

I eat fruit from the trees near my nest in the morning. I look for more food during the day.

I live with my family in a group called a flock. We talk to each other with loud croaks and barks.

I can not fly well with my small wings. Instead I hop between tree branches.

I live in the rainforest. I need high trees so I can make my home.

TOUCANS BY THE NUMBERS

Toucans lay up to **5 eggs** at a time.

There are about **35 different** species of toucans.

Toucans live in **Central** and **South America**.

Toucans live in groups of **6 birds or more**.

Toucans are **closely** related to **woodpeckers**.

A toucan's bill can be **four times** the size of its **head**.

KEY WORDS

Research has shown that as much as 65 percent of all written material published in English is made up of 300 words. These 300 words cannot be taught using pictures or learned by sounding them out. They must be recognized by sight. This book contains 51 common sight words to help young readers improve their reading fluency and comprehension. This book also teaches young readers several important content words, such as proper nouns. These words are paired with pictures to aid in learning and improve understanding.

Page	Sight Words First Appearance
4	a, am, I
7	and, for, known, large, my
8	be, can, help, its, keep, me, or, to, white
11	food, has, just, like, them, use
12	also, eat, sometimes
15	day, from, in, look, more, near, the, trees
16	each, family, group, live, other, talk, we, with
19	between, not, small, well
20	high, home, make, need, so

Page	Content Words First Appearance
4	toucan
7	bill, colors, tropical bird
11	edges, teeth
12	bird eggs, fruit, lizards, nuts, seeds
15	morning, nest
16	barks, croaks, flock
19	branches, wings
20	rainforest

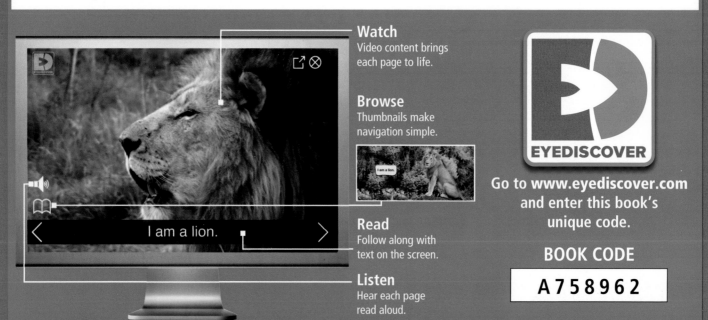

Watch
Video content brings each page to life.

Browse
Thumbnails make navigation simple.

Read
Follow along with text on the screen.

Listen
Hear each page read aloud.

I am a lion.

EYEDISCOVER

Go to www.eyediscover.com and enter this book's unique code.

BOOK CODE

A758962